AF270217

Gentoo Penguin

by Grace Hansen

abdobooks.com

Published by Abdo Kids, a division of ABDO, P.O. Box 398166, Minneapolis, Minnesota 55439.
Copyright © 2022 by Abdo Consulting Group, Inc. International copyrights reserved in all countries.
No part of this book may be reproduced in any form without written permission from the publisher.
Abdo Kids Jumbo™ is a trademark and logo of Abdo Kids.

Printed in the United States of America, North Mankato, Minnesota.

102021

012022

Photo Credits: Getty Images, iStock, Shutterstock

Production Contributors: Teddy Borth, Jennie Forsberg, Grace Hansen
Design Contributors: Candice Keimig, Victoria Bates

Library of Congress Control Number: 2021940125
Publisher's Cataloging-in-Publication Data

Names: Hansen, Grace, author.

Title: Gentoo penguin / by Grace Hansen

Description: Minneapolis, Minnesota : Abdo Kids, 2022 | Series: Antarctic animals | Includes online
   resources and index.

Identifiers: ISBN 9781098209391 (lib. bdg.) | ISBN 9781098260101 (ebook) | ISBN 9781098260453
   (Read-to-Me ebook)

Subjects: LCSH: Gentoo penguin--Juvenile literature. | Penguins--Juvenile literature. | Penguins--
   Behavior--Juvenile literature. | Zoology--Antarctica--Juvenile literature. | Antarctica--Juvenile literature.

Classification: DDC 591.709113--dc23

Table of Contents

Antarctica 4

Gentoo Penguins 6

Hunting & Food 16

Baby Gentoo Penguins 18

More Facts 22

Glossary 23

Index 24

Abdo Kids Code 24

Antarctica

Antarctica is the southernmost continent. Nearly all of Antarctica is covered by ice. It is one of the coldest, driest, and windiest places on Earth. But some amazing animals still live there!

5

Gentoo Penguins

Gentoo penguins live throughout much of the **southern hemisphere**. Many are found on the **Antarctic Peninsula** and the islands surrounding Antarctica.

Gentoo penguins live in **colonies**. There can be a few dozen to thousands of members in a colony.

Gentoo penguins grow
to be about 30 inches
(76 cm) tall. They weigh
around 12 pounds (5.4 kg).

Gentoo penguins have black and white feathers. Their faces are mostly black with white patches above the eyes. They also have bright orange beaks.

13

Gentoos are the fastest-swimming penguins. They can reach speeds of 22 miles per hour (35.4 kph). They can dive more than 600 feet (182 m) deep!

Hunting & Food

Gentoos spend their days
near the shore, ready to hunt.
While hunting **prey**, they can
stay underwater for up to
7 minutes. They like to eat fish,
squid, and **krill**.

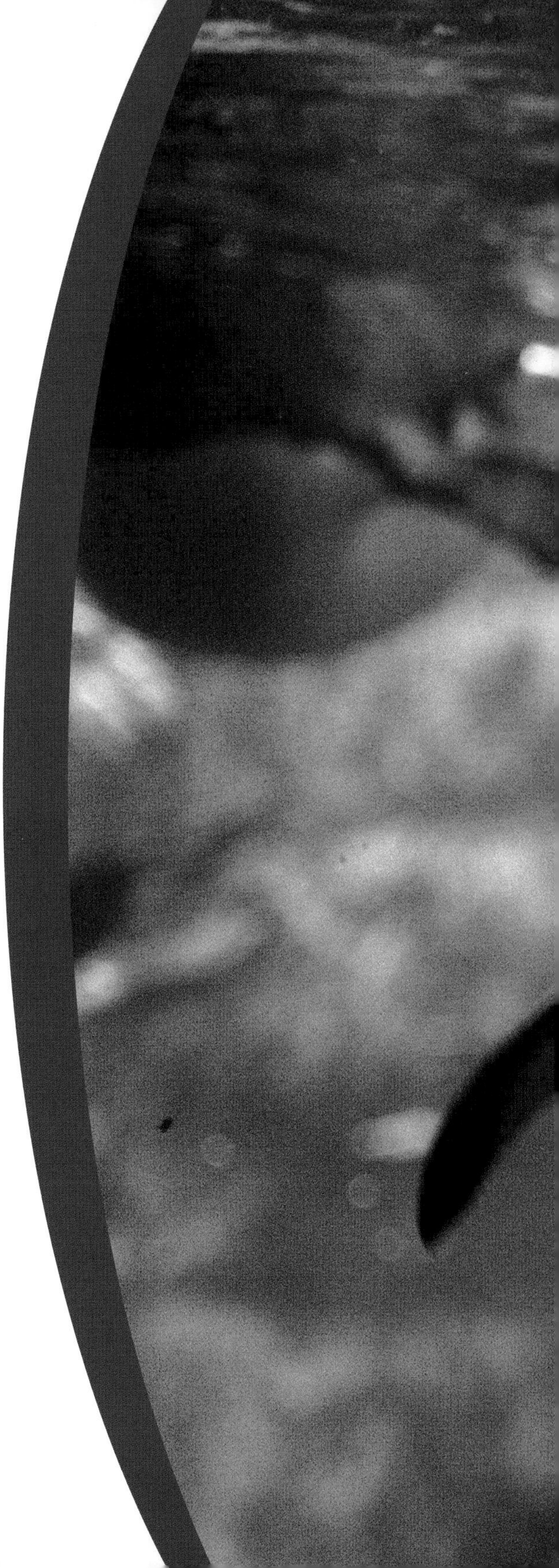

Baby Gentoo Penguins

Male and female gentoos come together to have young. They build nests made of stones, grass, and feathers. Females lay two white eggs. Parents take turns keeping the eggs warm.

After about 35 days, the
eggs hatch. Parents care for
the chicks for a month or so.
Then the chicks form **nursery**
groups. They stay together
until they have their feathers.

More Facts

- Gentoo penguins have longer tails than other kinds of penguins. As they walk, their tails sweep from side-to-side.

- Male gentoos attract females by bringing them gifts, like stones.

- Gentoos can make up to 450 dives a day for food!

Glossary

Antarctic Peninsula – the large piece of land that extends north off western Antarctica. It is about 800 miles (1300 km) long and the northernmost part of the continent.

colony – a group of animals of the same type living closely together.

krill – a very small, shrimplike animal that lives in the open seas.

nursery – a place where young animals gather to grow and be cared for.

prey – an animal that is hunted by another animal for food.

southern hemisphere – half of earth that is south of the equator.

Index

beak 12

chicks 20

colonies 8

coloring 12

diving 14, 16

eggs 18, 20

feathers 12, 18, 20

food 16

hunting 16

markings 12

nests 18

nurseries 20

range 6

size 10

speed 14

Visit **abdokids.com** to access crafts, games, videos, and more!